The Boy and The Cat

by

Canan Avsar

Illustrations by Sebastian Roslund

For Cansu and Can.

You are the light of my life.

Chapter I   The Cave

It was a cold and gloomy day. Aiden shivered as he strolled around the street although he was wearing his new, or better said, second hand new, thick jacket. The sky was dark with rain clouds and he could hear thunder rumbling a few miles away, while the wind was blowing around the corners. It was a bit of a scary day, not that Aiden would have been scared easily.

Normally he didn't mind a storm while sitting in his room and having a hot tea but somehow today the air seemed to smell very strongly of the storm and he could swear he was feeling the electricity in the air. He was walking around in his neighbourhood while kicking the debris out of his way. The little stones were crunching under his shoes and they would sometimes get stuck in his soles. There were no other noises apart from the ones he made himself – no people talking, no children laughing, no cars driving around.

Aiden was looking around to see if there was anything useful. Anything. He hadn't been very lucky lately in his "treasure hunt", as he called it. He was a bit distracted and that's when he saw a cat. A CAT! Aiden couldn't believe he was really seeing an animal, especially a cat. He had only ever seen a cat once and that was when he went to the zoo with his school and it didn't look like this one at all. That one had been a miserable little thing, behind bars, tiny, bony and scared. You could count its ribs, that's how starved it looked. There were not many animals in the zoo as most had died out. This cat, though, was bigger than the one in the zoo, and it had sand-coloured fur along with much bigger ears. Its eyes had such a distinctive form, and Aiden was reminded of the Egyptian cat statues he had seen at the museum. Aiden hurried after the cat and admired the beautiful and smooth movements of the animal. The cat walked almost elegantly through all the rubble and its small paws made no sound at all. Aiden tried to make no sounds as well but though he tried hard, he just seemed to not be able to do so – still, the cat didn't hear Aiden following it.

Aiden Reeves was 10 years old and he was skinny with knobbly knees. He had brown eyes, and light brown hair, and he was ill. Aiden had been born with a genetic disease, a deformation of his lungs that made it difficult for him to breathe. He lived together with his parents at the outskirts of the former metropolis New York City, in the year 3707. It was no metropolis anymore, as many people died and too few children were born. The bees died out in the 21st century and the effects on humanity were devastating. No one expected that their extinction would have such an impact all over the world. Fruits and flowers did not get pollinated, which meant that the production of food became very expensive and so the world started to suffer from hunger. To grow food without the bees, genetically modified crops were grown Many people died and the children who were born after this catastrophic incident were severely ill. They said that the loss of the bees had a wide impact not only on the pollination and the production of honey but the aftereffect was that the genetically modified crops affected humans. Children were born with genetic diseases. Families who were lucky enough to have money were able to save their children with the help of gene-therapy. The poorer families were not able to do this... The city was falling apart, and only Manhattan was well looked after as the rich people lived there. Aiden had only been in Manhattan a few times: once, when his parents brought him to a hospital to see a doctor, the other times with the

school, to visit the Central Park Zoo and again
when they went to the Metropolitan Museum of
Art to see an Egyptian history exhibition.

Those times, he couldn't stop looking around
at all the lights, which had been turned on already
(as it was afternoon and because it was winter) and
they were shining so brightly that at times he had
to squint his eyes; the shops were so full of
colourful things he had never seen before, as if all
the brightness and beauty of the world was centred
in these windows; there were elegant people
wearing clothes in bright colours like red, yellow
and blue and in a style he had never seen in the
outskirts before; and the noises of the cars, with
their roaring motors and the honking of their
horns, and the music coming out of the shops, with
the bass thumping right through his ears, echoed in
his brain until he felt overwhelmed and dizzy. The
delicious smell of food he never had tried was
floating through the streets and made his mouth
water: while he looked at the chocolates and
bonbons in the window shops he felt a kind of

desperation, as he knew that his family never would be able to afford to buy such luxurious sweets.

Anyways, Aiden lived in the outskirts of New York city, and there you didn't have much light as the electricity was limited to a few hours in the evening. The people were already used to the darkness. Nearly all of the buildings were abandoned and only the street in which he lived with his family was inhabited, by them and a few other people. Candles were too expensive as there were no bees to produce the wax anymore. Darkness was a permanent state. Aiden was the only child and his parents were a bit too protective for his taste sometimes. Not that they would cover him in cotton wool, but he would get reminded the whole time that he should be careful, which he found completely unnecessary and a bit annoying, as he obviously wasn't a baby anymore. There were also only a few children here he could play with, due to the fact that babies were rarely born to the poorer families.

The streets were riddled with holes as the weeds had forced their way through the asphalt, and debris from the buildings was lying around everywhere. The families who lived here were the poorest of the poorest in NYC, but they tried their best to look after each other. Often they would share their food or water and if any of them was lucky enough to find something useful like a pack of vegetable seeds, they would always share instead of keeping it to themselves. Each of the families tried to increase their food by planting fruits, herbs and vegetables in their little allotments, but seeds were a rarity and very expensive.

Aiden would sometimes roam around in his neighbourhood after school, while his parents were both working in the factory in Manhattan. They worked hard, as they were trying to get the money together for Aidan's therapy. Most days he just walked around in the neighbourhood and looked to see if he could find anything useful lying around in the streets. He liked to find things that the whole family could use, like a pot for cooking or, one of his most valuable treasures, a book. Aiden loved books and one of the happiest days in his life was when he was able to read a short story for his mum, for the first time ever.

He had to be careful not to run. It wasn't that he wouldn't have liked to run around, climb up trees, or play chase in school with the other kids – it was that his condition did not allow him to, as he would already be short of breath after a few meters, and that's why he was only walking. Aiden also knew that he was not allowed to go into the abandoned buildings, his parents had told him this more than once, as the danger of them falling apart, at any time, was too high.

Aiden just couldn't hold himself back, and he followed the cat as it was walking into the front yard of an abandoned church. Some of the gravestones here were broken or were laying flat on the soil, and seemed to be scattered all over the place. He tried not to make too much noise while he was carefully walking over the debris. He

hesitated just for a second about whether he should
go after the cat, but with a little shake of his head
he followed it as it was wedging through the small
gap of the left-open-and-stuck door into the
church.

The moment he pushed open the door a bit
further to squeeze in and enter the building he saw
a white light, his head spun and he closed his eyes
tight to block out the blinding light. The moment
he opened his eyes, he saw something that looked
like the entrance of a cave, a wide desert in the
distance and a settlement at the foot of the

mountain he was looking down from. He breathed in heavily and the cat turned around startled, looked surprised at Aiden and said, "What on earth are you doing here?" And then, he saw nothing but the empty blackness of his mind.

Aiden felt cold, damp stone under his body and hands when he regained consciousness. He smelled moldy, dry air and slowly opened his eyes. The bright light falling on him was blinding his eyes and he shrieked with surprise when he heard an arrogant voice.

"Thank the Goddess Bastet you're awake. I thought you'd never wake up."

The boy sat up slowly and looking around he was surprised to see that he was in the cave. He looked panicked at the strange, talking cat and tried to crawl backwards away from it without letting it out of his view, though he didn't get far, as he reached the walls of the cave after a few seconds. A hot desert wind blew into the cave and took the boy's breath away. The sun shone so bright outside that although Aiden was sitting in the cave he had to squint his eyes when he looked outside. He never had seen such a bright sun before. The cat did look different than the cats Aiden had seen at the zoo or in books. Its eyes were almond like, and its legs were much longer and thinner than the legs of the cats Aiden knew of. The cat's sand-coloured short fur was disrupted by dark brown streaks on its head and its paws. Aiden looked fascinated at the cat and couldn't avert his gaze from this beautiful creature.

The cat started licking its paw while it glanced over at the boy.

"Do you think we can talk now without you fainting? I have a few errands to run and your presence here is most inconvenient."

It sounded more than annoyed, and spoke with a light purr in its voice.

Aiden blinked again.

Then the cat said,

"You can speak?" said Aiden, and the cat answered, "Well obviously you're not a very bright one, are you?"

"I've never met a cat that talks."

"Of course not – we usually keep that to ourselves."

"You mean all cats can speak?"

"Now, never mind that, we have more urgent problems than us cats speaking. What do you want? Who are you? And why are you here?"

Aiden was a bit surprised by the questions and couldn't do anything other than blink.

His mouth was wide open until the cat asked again.

"Don't sit here like a statue, give me an answer you silly boy."

Aiden got a bit annoyed now himself. He impatiently brushed his hand through his hair.

"I'm not a silly boy. And by the way, I was just following you as I have never seen a cat in my neighbourhood, and when I stepped into the church I came out here, and..."

The cat nearly yelled.

"Wait, wait! Are you telling me you followed me? By the Goddess Bastet, this is not good, not good at all... I'll get so many problems with the head of my order for this... I should've been more careful but I was so busy thinking..."

The cat started mumbling to itself and Aiden couldn't understand anything. He asked the cat, who was pacing and mumbling,

"Listen, where am I? This does not look like my neighbourhood – I've never been in a cave and maybe I've hit my head somehow and I'm now lying with a head wound somewhere in the dirt, bleeding to death..."

The cat stopped mumbling and looked Aiden straight in the eye and said dryly

"This is not your neighbourhood, there is not even a street here. We are not even in your time. We are in Egypt. To be precise it's Ancient Egypt, as you would call it."

Aiden jumped up and tried to run out of the cave entrance but with an elegant jump the cat blocked his way.

"Wait! You can't just run out of here! What do you think the people from this time would do to you? They would think you are a demon or a sorcerer and in minutes you'd get captured, jailed, or worse, enslaved!"

Aiden sunk down again at the floor. He couldn't believe what the cat was saying and this was probably just a bad dream or maybe he really did hit his head somewhere and was now having a hallucination. But despite the blinking and the shaking of his head, the cat still didn't disappear and Aiden was still not back in his street.

"Ok, let's get this straight. You are a talking cat. I am in Egypt and this is not even my time. Is that correct so far?"

"Exactly. Now could you please calm down so we can look at our options?"

"Sure. Go on then. What are we going to do? How do I get back home and why can't I just walk back in to the cave and get home?"

Aiden started shaking but at this time it was not because he was cold, it was because he was scared.

"The problem is, that the time portal is closed now, which means you are trapped here."

"Trapped? You mean forever?"

Aiden felt panic rising.

"Well, not exactly. We can open the time portal again but that will take a while as it is quite complicated and I have to inform the head of my order to get permission to open the time portal –

which will get me into a lot of trouble, I can tell you that."

"What are you waiting for then? Let's go and tell your boss or whoever he is and get me home. My mum and dad are surely worried sick already. Please, help me get home."

Aiden looked very distressed and his face was pale,

"Of course I will help you but you have put me in quite a difficult position and I have to be careful not to upset the head. You really shouldn't have followed me."

"It wasn't as if I would've known what was going to happen, you know?" Aiden replied annoyed.

The cat started to walk up and down the entrance of the cave as if the movement helped it to think better. It stopped its pacing and looked outside into the light and toward the settlement which could be seen a bit in the distance.

"Maybe I should try to get you clothes and then I can take you into the city to meet the head. Please, do stay here, do not go anywhere as you would be in mortal danger, and wait till I'm back. I promise I will take care of you and bring you safe home again. It's my fault that you are here and I will put everything right again."

With these words, the cat just left Aiden scared and alone and he had to sit down on the floor before he fainted. Again.

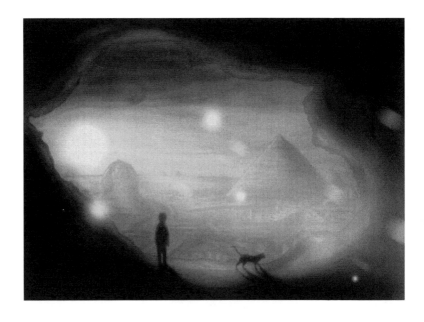

Chapter II   Akila

While Aiden waited for the cat, he looked around at the cave. It seemed to be a worshipping place as there was an altar at the back of the cave with cat statues standing on each side of it. Apart from that, the cave was quite empty. Aiden got a bit agitated as he was waiting for the cat to come back and he sat at the entrance of the cave and looked out at the settlement. He could see people walking with baskets on their heads and others leading cows and horses through the streets. Unfortunately he was too far away to see their faces but he already had spotted a few children who seemed to play and run around. That made him a bit envious but he forgot that feeling very fast as he was too fascinated by seeing so many children. Most of the little ones seemed to be completely nude and he wondered why they were not wearing any clothes.

Meanwhile the cat was on its way to the town and every man, woman and child was careful to make space for it. The cat was used to the somewhat awestruck behaviour of the people and did not waste a single moment on it. It saw from the corner of its eyes a man turning around a corner and was wondering for a moment if it hadn't seen that man just a few streets earlier. Shaking off that thought, it moved quietly to a side street where it knew the laundry quarter of the town was. Somehow it couldn't get rid of the feeling that there was something wrong...

The cat looked around at the laundry that was being washed and dried here but realised very quickly that it needed help to get some clothes for the boy. It should have thought of that earlier but sometimes the cat forgot that it was so small – and it was a bit inconvenient to be a cat when it came to carrying things that were bigger than a kitten. It was obviously not able to carry big things like a pile of clothes. But how could the cat get anyone to help it? While it turned around to look for any inspiration it saw a little girl hiding behind a corner of the laundry tubs. She was small, maybe 9 years old, and she looked as if she hadn't had anything proper to eat for a while. Her hair was in streaks and her hands and her face were dark from dirt. The cat looked around to see if there were any other people nearby. When the cat was sure that it was alone with the girl, it walked towards her and started to speak. The girl gasped for air and fainted.

"Why for the love of Ra do these humans faint the whole time?"

The cat looked irritated and sat down to clean its fur until the girl awoke again.

Meanwhile Aiden was waiting in the cave and was really worried that the cat wouldn't come back, and that he was going to be stuck in the past forever. He was a bit annoyed at himself because he did exactly what his parents told him not to do.

"Don't go into the buildings. It's not safe."

He was sure that they hadn't thought in their wildest dreams of the dangers of time travel when they had warned him from entering abandoned buildings.

Aiden never was very interested in history at school and wished now he would have paid a bit more attention. He was trying to remember what he knew about Ancient Egypt and had to admit to himself that there was not much apart from the pyramids and the mummies. He did find the mummies interesting, a bit spooky, but anyways that was about all he could remember.

The sun looked past noon and he wondered what time it was, and whether the cat would keep its promise to come back soon. He was starting to get thirsty in this hot weather and his breathing got a bit worse than usual...

The cat got a bit impatient while it was waiting for the girl to regain consciousness, but it knew that it needed the girl's help to get clothes for Aiden. After a few minutes the girl awoke and she looked frightened as soon as her eyes fell on the cat. Before she could faint again, or worse, yell, the cat tried to speak calmly to her.

"Listen, don't be scared. I know this is a bit much for you but I need your help. Promise me that you won't scream and that you will do as I ask you."

The child was too confused to answer and she just nodded with her head.

"Very well then. Look, I need to get clothes for a boy, around your age, maybe a bit taller and you have to come with me and carry the clothes for me. Do you understand?"

The girl still wasn't answering and was just sitting there like a statue.

"Are you hungry? How about this? You help me, and I will get you something to eat. Deal?"

"Akila."

"What?"

"My name is Akila. And I am very hungry."

The cat tried not to laugh and gave her a nod.

"Well, Akila, in that case let's go and get the clothes for the boy so we can get you something to eat."

Akila stood up and looked at the cat.

"You haven't told me your name."

"I am Sekhemib, the powerful at heart."

"You are such a beautiful kitty."

"Excuse me? I am a male cat, not a kitty!" Sekhemib answered, offended.

Akila blushed and apologised for this affront.

"Apology accepted," he answered.

And with this, the unlikely pair went on to find a few clothes for Aiden.

Aiden got quite agitated while he was waiting for the cat and couldn't stop himself looking outside the cave to see it was coming back. It was afternoon already and his thirst started to bother him. Then he saw a little figure coming up the path to the cave. Accompanying it was the cat and they moved in unison towards the cave. The boy couldn't hold himself back and stormed out of the cave.

"I thought you wouldn't come back."

"I told you that I would. I promised. This is Akila by the way, and she is being so generous as to help us."

"Hello Akila, I am Aiden."

The girl looked bewildered at Aidan's hand, which he stretched out to shake hers.

"My dear boy, your customs of the future are not known in this time."

Aiden frowned and took back his hand and ran his hand through his hair ,which he used to do when he felt insecure. Meanwhile the girl opened up the bundle she was carrying and said,

"You don't look like you are from around here"

"Why do I understand Akila, by the way?" asked Aiden of the irritated cat, before answering her.

"Goodness me. It's a side effect of the time travel, of course, everyone knows that." Sekhemib responded with a drawling voice.

Then the cat answered Akila before Aiden could.

"He is not."

"Where are you from then?"

Again the cat interrupted before the boy could answer her question.

"I don't think you need to know that."

Aiden was so distressed now that he cried out,

"You know what? I am a bit tired and thirsty and to be honest, I am quite concerned that I won't get back to my time. So could you please stop playing the mysterious card and let us just make a plan for how I can get home again? Please?"

"What do you mean with your time?"

Akila's eyes were wide open and her face showed a curiosity that Aiden recognised in himself whenever he thought that he had found a riddle he could solve and in which he was interested.

The cat and Aiden spoke at the same time.

"I am from the future."

"He is from the future."

Akila didn't even blink when they revealed this to her.

"I always knew that there was magic."

The cat sighed impatiently.

"Actually it's a combination of science with universal energy, but you wouldn't understand it anyway. Never mind that now. We have to sit down and make a plan for how we are going to open the time portal again. And the much more urgent question is, how we are going to hide Aiden for a whole week..."

"A whole WEEK? You didn't tell me that I have to wait a whole week! My parents will be worried sick when I'm not at home on time!" Aiden was nearly yelling.

The cat tried to calm Aiden down. "Look, it takes time to open the portal. We need ingredients and I have to get the permission from the head of the temple to open it. I promise I'll get you home again but for now we need a place for you to stay."

"Well, Akila, do you have a place where I could stay?" asked Aiden.

The girl looked embarrassed and hung her head, ashamed.

"I'm very sorry but I am looking for somewhere to stay myself..."

"Don't you have a family?"

"My family is dead. They died around 3 weeks ago. I have been living on the streets since then."

"But don't you have anywhere else to stay? Extended family? Family friends?"

Akila just shook her head.

"Great. Now I have two kids to look after..." mumbled the grumpy cat.

Akila and Aiden looked at each other with shared irritation when the cat turned around and stared out of the cave.

"My biggest problem is, how I am going to tell the head of my order that I didn't succeed in fulfilling his command? Not to mention the fact that I brought back a little boy from the future just because I wasn't careful."

Chapter III   The Circus

Sekhemib told the children to stay in the cave
while he went to speak with his order's head. It
was already late afternoon and the children were
not happy about having to stay in the cave without
food and water. Though Sekhemib promised to
organise something to eat, they were too hungry to
follow his instruction to wait. So, when the cat was
gone, they decided that one of them would go to
look for water and food. As Akila was the one with
knowledge of the area, she went to get everything
they needed, or to be precise, to beg for and
possibly steal it.

Aiden was, again, just sitting and waiting in
the cave and he felt very helpless. Meanwhile he
tried to keep himself occupied by putting on the
clothes which Akila and the cat brought him. They
were in a very simple cut and when he put the
clothes on he felt quite uncomfortable. Not only
were they in a very unknown style for Aiden, the
fabric was also very scratchy, though they seemed

to instantly make him feel cooler. He thought he should ask Akila what kind of fabric this was.

The clothes Akila and Sekhemib brought him were only a temporary distraction. Again, he had nothing to do and he thought of his family and what they would do if they didn't find him at home waiting for them. He always tried to be careful when wandering around in the city, as he knew that it could be dangerous with all the debris lying around. His parents trusted him to be considerate enough to take care of himself and he was sure that they would be very worried if he wasn't at home in time.

While Aiden waited impatiently for Akila and Sekhemib to come back, Akila had a real surprise upon returning to the town. To her amazement, a wandering circus had arrived while she was at the cave and it was just starting to unload the camels and carts of heavy baggage. Men and women were running around, trying to organise the unloading while making space for the tents to be put up. Akila couldn't stop looking at the company in awe while the noises of the animals' roaring and grunting mixed with the mens' ordering and shouting, when she had an idea. Immediately she went to one of the men who seemed to be the boss as he was ordering the others around to unload the carts and to look after the animals.

"Excuse me please, but do you by any chance need help, as my cousin and I are looking for work. We can work hard and we are both very reliable," the little girl told the tall man earnestly.

The man had a dark face with an impressive black beard and was wearing a colourful cape. He looked down at the girl with his sparkly brown eyes and his face changed from annoyed to amused at the sight of the little, skinny girl with the dirty face.

"Can you feed the lions? Or the crocodile? What about the snakes?"

Akila had to swallow a bit but she held up her chin and answered him bravely.

"Yes, yes I can do that. I am not scared."

The man smiled at her determination and pulled her aside as one of the men passed with a huge elephant.

"Alright then. You get something to eat twice a day and a place to sleep. No money. Understood?"

"Yes. Understood."

Akila's eyes were glowing with happiness. She had found a job and a place to stay for herself and Aiden.

As fast as possible, she ran back to the cave temple to get to Aiden and tell him the good news. She couldn't wait to see his surprised face and was chuckling happily as she imagined it.

When Akila came running back to the cave, Aiden feared the worst. What if the people of the city had found out about him? What if they came to capture him? He started to get ready to run off, when Akila arrived at the cave and breathlessly tried to tell him something.

"We... I... work... lions..."

She was so out of breath that she needed a few minutes to catch it again so that she could speak.

"Please could you repeat what you said? I haven't understood anything, I'm afraid."

"Alright: I found work for us."

"Work? What work? You were supposed to get something to eat and drink, not work!"

Akila wrinkled her nose at Aidan's outburst and put her little hands on her skinny hips.

"You know what? This is the best I could do. We will get something to eat twice a day and we will have a safe place to sleep. That is much more than I had the last few weeks and I'm going to take this chance whether you join me or not!"

Aidan felt sorry for his lack of gratitude but he wasn't sure if this whole work thing would be a good idea.

Sekhemib meanwhile had gone to the temple of Bastet in the city to meet the head of his order. The cat didn't feel very good about the news he was going to give, but tried to rehearse what he was going to say.

"I'm very sorry master but I haven't been successful finding the artifact. I have also made a huge mistake. I was inattentive when going back to the time portal and a young boy followed me. I will make it right again, master. I am solely responsible for this mess. Please forgive me, master."

The temple had its own lake, outside the enclosure, where the priests would bring their offerings to the gods and hold holy ceremonies because the lake received its water directly from the sacred river Nile. The temple's finances came from its farmlands, which were responsible for the production of grains and fruits for the care of herds of livestock.

When Sekhemib arrived at the entrance of the temple, the cat stopped and breathed heavily, in and out, to calm his nerves. Then he walked bravely through the door, but felt a bit like he was entering a lion's den.

Sekhemib entered the temple and the fires in the oil lamps cast eerie shadows over the walls and pillars. The cat thought that it could be a sign as to how the talk with his master was going to go. The cat was feeling worse from minute to minute and he tried to push the meeting as far away as possible by strolling through the temple. At this time of the day were not many humans worshipping here and only the priests were allowed to enter the most sacred part of the temple, the sanctuary. None of the priests were paying attention to the cat, they were just going about their usual business. The further Sekhemib went into the temple, the more nervous he became. Before he could change his mind regarding whether to enter the sanctuary, he saw a man coming out of it. Not only was this a sacrilege, as only the priests had permission to enter the sanctuary, but he could have sworn that he had seen that man already today, following him through the streets. Sekhemib couldn't explain what it was, but he felt more than just scared of the reaction of his master: his intuition told him that there was something wrong here.

When the temple cat got back to the cave, he was surprised by the news of the children having found work and a somewhere to stay. Sekhemib wasn't very happy about this development but he was also aware that the kids really needed a place, for a while. It could also become a place to stay, for Akila, for a longer period. She was alone and needed a home. The cat felt responsible for the little girl, as it was his fault that she had gotten involved in the whole story.

The three of them got ready but, before they left the cave to walk to the town together, they tried to cover Aidan's skin and hair with dirt. Sekhemib was worried that Aidan would draw unwanted attention from slave traders and wanted to make sure that he would blend in with everyone else. They agreed to meet near the fountain at the market place every evening at eight, as they had to keep in mind that they needed to gather the ingredients for the time portal so Aidan could get back to his own time again.

Aidan and Akila went on to the circus. Both were chatting happily about seeing the animals and were looking forward to watching the show. When Aidan and Akila arrived at the campsite of the circus, Akila seemed to not be at all impressed by the sight of the tents and the animals roaring, grunting and trumpeting, but Aidan's eyes were glistening with excitement when he saw these beautiful creatures. The smell of the animals was so intense, that, combined with the heat, Aidan had the feeling that he was going to faint due to that and all the visions his brain had to process. He couldn't get enough and turned his head from one side to the other as if he didn't want to miss one little thing.

The children went on to the ringmaster to introduce Aidan and to ask what their tasks would be. Although they had tried to disguise Aidan a bit, the big, bearded man was very astonished to see a child with such white skin. But he tried to hide his

surprise and sent them to the camels to help feed
and look after them.

"Go over there to the camels. Help Senbi to
feed them and ask him for further tasks, he will tell
you."

The children ran hand in hand to the direction
the ringmaster showed them and went directly to
the only man who was with the camels. Senbi was
an old and grey haired man, his face so full of
wrinkles that his skin looked nearly as rough as the
skin of the elephants the children saw from afar. He
seemed to be a nice fellow, with a soft spot for
animals and children. Patiently he explained to the
kids what they had to do and how to avoid the
sometimes painful bites of the camels in case they
were in a bad mood. The time flew by in an instant
and soon it was evening. A nice smell of food
floated over the circus area and the children's
stomachs made such loud noises that even Senbi
could hear it. He sent the kids away, laughing at
their excitement, to get something to eat, and
followed them shortly afterwards. Akila and Aidan

got in line like everyone else and soon they got a bowl of something mushy, a big slice of bread and a mug full of some kind of fluid. Aidan looked very suspiciously at everything and asked Akila what it was. She looked very happy about the food and drank and chatted happily,

"This is bread, made out of emmer wheat. Don't you have bread in your time?"

"Shhhh. Don't speak so loud." Aiden looked scared.

"We have to be careful. I want to survive this whole story, you know."

Akila looked embarrassed and answered,

"Sorry, I forgot for a moment. Well, what you have in the mug is beer, and it is made from barley, and it is so nutritious that you could even survive on it, without eating anything else, though I'm really happy to get a bowl of stew. I haven't had any the last few weeks since my parents died."

Both children went very quiet when Akila spoke about it, and ate their meal in silence.

Sekhemib, in the meantime, went back to the temple. He didn't tell the kids that the conversation with the head of his order had gone quite badly. Not only did he get scolded for his inattentiveness, but Sekhemib knew very well the dangers of time travel. There were a few rules he had known since he was a kitten: first, do not talk with humans; second, make sure no one sees you when entering the time portal; and third, never allow a human to enter the time portal. It seemed that he, in just one day, had broken all three rules...

Sekhemib tried to be calm when he entered the sanctuary to meet the order of his head again. He wasn't looking forward to telling him that the children were now working at the circus, but it was surely better than having them in the temple.

The cat quietly entered the most sacred room in the temple and was surprised to see that the head was not here. He rarely left the sanctuary and Sekhemib was not sure what the reason for his absence could be. Should he wait here or should he come back later? He was undecided, but maybe he would find the head outside, so he left the sanctuary and strolled out of the temple.

And there he saw him. The head of the order was standing at the temple lake and was speaking with the guy Sekhemib had now seen a few times today. What was going on? The cat was getting quite suspicious. Not only was this whole situation unusual but in addition the way his head had spoken with him at their first meeting today was completely out of order. Sekhemib was not only scolded but witnessed an attitude in his head that he had never seen before. His head had gotten extremely angry and for a split second Sekhemib thought that he was going to attack him when he told him about the children. Another thing that had irritated the cat even more was that his head had shown more interest in Akila than in Aiden, as if he knew something about her already.

The temple cat fought an inner battle with himself regarding whether he should go to try to find out what was going on. Should he listen in on these two? Should he respect his head, trust his decisions and follow just his orders? Was he not responsible for the children? With who was his allegiance now? And then he thought of the scared faces of the children and his decision was final. Very quietly he moved behind the bushes that were planted around the lake and tried to get near the unlikely pair.

"Holy master, I have failed you."

The cat's claws could be seen and he asked the man with a sneering voice,

"What do you mean, you failed me? Was the order I gave you too complicated for you? I only expected you to get the girl. How is it possible to lose a child?"

"Master, she has been hiding the last few weeks after the death of her parents..."

" I am aware of that you useless idiot. I need the girl! You have to bring her to me. As soon as possible. I'm running out of time."

"Master, it is a bit difficult now to get her when she is surrounded by so many people. The circus people are very protective of their kind and as they took the kid in they won't let her go so easily."

"I don't care how difficult it is! You are solely responsible for this whole mess and I expect you to sort it out!"

"Yes master. I will."

The man hung his head and made a bow before he turned around and left the temple. While the master still stood at the lake caught in his thoughts, Sekhemib was feeling shocked. Did this really just happen? Did he really just hear the master giving orders to kidnap Akila? It must have been Akila as she and Aiden were the only children joining the circus today. What was going on here? Why was Akila in danger? This didn't sound good at all...

Chapter IV   The Oasis

The children meanwhile felt much better after having a nutritious meal, and they were strolling around the circus camp. Aiden couldn't believe his eyes, and felt so happy to see all the animals he mainly knew from books, but in reality they were much more interesting. His favourites were the monkeys, with the tricks they were showing. They made him laugh and he just wished his parents could see these beautiful creatures.

Akila seemed to be very happy as well. It was the first time for three weeks that she had had a full stomach. The kids even got a little tent for themselves to sleep in and Akila would have at least the coming night to sleep without being in danger. As a girl it was particularly dangerous to sleep rough, not only because of the danger of being picked up by the slave-traders but also because of the stray dogs. They were always looking for food and a little girl was just their taste.

It was nearly eight o'clock and the sun went down so fast that Aiden was very surprised by the darkness that fell over the camp. The circus people started to tidy everything up as they had an exhausting day ahead of them, having their presentations the next day. Slowly, everyone was going back to their tents after checking on the animals one last time. The kids said good night to everyone and went to their tents. They were planning on quietly sneaking away to meet Sekhemib at the well.

It went quiet in the camp, people going to sleep after a hard day's work, and only the animals could be heard grunting and shoving each other.

Akila and Aiden were sitting in their tent in complete darkness. They were whispering about which way they should sneak out without raising any suspicion.

Before the children could get out of their tent, two men jumped inside, grabbed the kids, covered their mouths and dragged them out of the tent. Aiden tried to break free and tried to kick and punch the man who was holding him, but he was just too small, and it didn't help that he was already exhausted from his day. Only a few meters away was another man waiting with four camels, and they tied up the kids together on one camel. They threatened the children, if they should dare to scream for help, and both Akila and Aiden heard how serious the men were: and off they rode at an excessive speed, as if they were running away from something.

The children were very scared and, though they were together, the men got angry when they tried to speak with each other. They had ties on their hands and their feet were tied onto the camel so even if they wriggled their hands free they still wouldn't have been able to run. The night sky was beautiful, Aiden had never seen so many stars before, and without any clouds obscuring the full moon it was shining so brightly that there was no need for any other light source. Akila's eyes were so big that Aiden felt the need to comfort her and he grabbed her hand to hold it tight. Akila was getting tired and her head was falling from one side to the other even though she tried to stay awake. It seemed like the journey was going on the whole night, but, soon after midnight, they saw an oasis in the distance with palm trees, a little water lake and tents. The kids looked at each other worriedly and didn't know what fate was awaiting them.

Sekhemib, meanwhile, needed a few minutes to get out of his catharsis. He stood there, paralysed. Suddenly he thought,

"Akila! And Aiden! I have to warn them! They're in danger! I have to hurry to the circus!"

But before he could hurry back to the town his master caught him.

"Sekhemib! What are you doing here?"

Sekhemib came out quietly from behind the bush and tried to stroll casually over to his master.

"Greetings holy master. I was looking for you and when I couldn't see you in the sanctuary, I went out to look for you. It is a beautiful evening for a little walk, isn't it?"

"Indeed it is, dear friend. How long have you been here?"

The master tried to sound uninterested but somehow his voice sounded strained and Sekhemib was aware that he had to be very careful now with what he was going to say.

"I just arrived when you saw me master. I was looking for a mouse that I thought ran behind the bush. You know how fond I am of a nice little hunt."

"Well, well. Let us go inside and discuss the problems you made, dear Sekhemib."

"Master, could we not postpone our conversation?"

The master closed its eyes into slits and answered in a sneering voice

"You do as I order you, Sekhemib. You have failed me already today and I am expecting you to sort this mess out. And now, follow me."

Sekhemib had no choice but to follow his master or he would have raised his masters' suspicions. He just hoped that he wouldn't be late for his meeting with the children.

Chapter V   The Cave

When Sekhemib arrived at the well and realised that it was already after the time he and the children had agreed to meet up and the kids weren't there, he got a very bad feeling. What should he do? Should he wait a little longer? He considered: if he was to waste time and the children were in danger, he wouldn't be helping them at all. What could a little cat do anyway? Sekhemib started pacing around the well and tried to think through his options. Wait here or look for the children at the circus camp? And what should he do if they were not there? The cat got more desperate from minute to minute and at last made the decision to go look for the children.

As the circus camp was outside of town, Sekhemib needed a few minutes to reach it, although he ran as fast as he could. His intuition told him that the children wouldn't forget to meet him and that the only reason for them not to come at the agreed time was that they couldn't. He was almost certain that there could only be one reason why they didn't show up: he was too late and the children must have already been abducted.

Sekhemib found the tent of the kids without any problems, as he was following their scent. When he looked inside his worst nightmare came true. The children were gone. Nothing was in there. Not even the tiniest clue about what had happened. The cat sniffed around like a dog but he couldn't make out anything apart from the kids odour and a scent of camels – but maybe that came over from the circus camels? What should he do now?

Meanwhile, Akila and Aiden had been taken off the camels and, though their hands were still tied up, they could at least walk on their own feet. The camel journey was much more exhausting than Aiden would have imagined, with all the shaking, but Akila looked worse than him. This day had taken a huge toll on her and she looked as if she would faint anytime soon.

The children were pushed forward and taken into a huge tent where a fire was lit in the middle and the smoke was escaping through a hole above it. An elderly man was sitting there, cracking nuts. Aiden had never seen a man like him. His hair and beard was completely white and his face was riddled with wrinkles, and he had eyes of such striking blue colour that Aiden couldn't hold himself back and was staring at the man.

After putting the nuts aside he looked at the group and asked,

"How was your journey, children?"

Aiden was surprised with the question and didn't know what to answer, but Akila seemed to have gained a bit of her courage back.

"It would have been better if we had been invited properly."

The old man started chuckling amusedly and waved them to come over.

"What a brave little girl you are. Tell me, what is your name?"

"I am called Akila."

"And your friend?"

"Aiden, my name is Aiden."

Aiden tried to look as feisty and brave as Akila, and looked the man straight in the eyes.

"Well, Aiden and Akila, you are our guests for a while. You get permission to walk freely around here, but I warn you, don't try to run away. There are enough snakes and other dangers in the desert that you would die in a few hours if you tried to run off. You can go to sleep now and we will talk in the morning."

With a nod with his head he sent the kids and the men away. They were pushed around again, and again they got a little tent for themselves. The children were so exhausted that they couldn't even find the energy to speak about the whole situation. They fell asleep on the carpets on the floor, holding hands, as both had the feeling that they only had each other for comfort.

Early in the morning the children were woken up and again brought to the old nomad. They were still holding hands and this did not escape the man's gaze. The children were standing in the same tent as last night but this time the old man was not alone. Another man was with him, a gruff looking man with dark hair and a scar on his face.

Aiden and Akila were pushed in front of the man again and Aiden looked angrily over his shoulder at the man shoving him. The old man cleared his throat and Aiden turned his head again.

"Good morning, dear friends. Did you get a good rest? I hope my men were not too rough on the both of you." He laughed as if he had made a good joke.

The children didn't answer. They did not let go of each other's hands and did not show any signs of being scared, although Aiden could feel Akila's hand tremble.

"Well, my little guests, we have a small request to make. Our employer wishes us to get information from you, very specific information."

"What kind of information is this?" Aiden asked confused.

"Not from you, my friend, I'm afraid. An item of information from your girlfriend," the old man answered in earnest.

"From me?" Akila quietly asked.

"Yes, my little princess, from you. You know the location of an important place. And our employer wishes to know the exact location of it: the grave."

"A grave? I don't know what you mean. The village graveyard is at the outskirts of the village, everyone knows that."

Akila's eyes were huge with surprise while looking at the old man. She had no idea what he was talking about and looked questioningly at Aiden.

The old man looked suspiciously at the girl while he was stroking his long, grey beard. He didn't say a word but was just watching the kids as if he was lost in his thoughts.

Sekhemib, meanwhile, went back to the cave with the shrine as he hoped that the kids might have run away and hidden in there – but the cave was empty. The cat was so worried and scared that he just moved in front of the shrine and started praying.

"Goddess Bastet, I am your humble servant, please, hear my pleas. My dear little friends, two children, are vanished and I have no idea where to start to look for them. I beg you, almighty, help me."

And with these words he fell asleep in front of the goddess statue.

The children, in the hands of the nomads, tried to be brave. The old man started to ask Akila question after question, and she answered them as well as she could. During the interrogation, Aiden found out that Akila's parents and her brother did not die a natural death but that they had been murdered. He wondered why Akila had not told him this, but guessed that she was just scared and still too grief-stricken to share this with him, someone who was practically a stranger. Although the adventures of the last 18 hours had brought them together, they just had not had the time to know each other properly. It seemed like time was passing by so fast that Aiden wondered if that was a side effect of the time travel itself or if his perception of time had changed because of the excitement of the last few hours.

"So your parents were working for the Pharaoh and helped him to prepare his mausoleum for him, is that right?" the old man tried to summarise the information he got from Akila.

"Yes." she answered.

"And they took you to the location of the mausoleum when they were working there, is that also right?"

"Yes." answered Akila again.

"So you could show me where the mausoleum is, couldn't you?"

"I guess so, but I only ever went there from the city. I can't find the way from here."

The old man looked very pleased and after a little nod to one of his men, he got up from his seat.

"Well, well, my little friends. It seems like we are making a small trip now."

And with these words the children were pulled out of the tent and put on a camel again. As the last time they sat on a camel was dark, the kids hadn't been aware until now of the beautiful scenery surrounding them – but they couldn't enjoy it at this time anyways.

The journey to the city didn't take long and after a few hours they could already see the temple buildings from afar. Aiden and Akila couldn't talk with each other but Akila squeezed Aiden's hand a few times during the ride, which gave him the hope that she had a little plan. He couldn't think of anything himself – what could two little kids do anyway? But he also didn't want to give up. Giving up was not in his nature, and, as he knew of Akila now, not in hers either.

Akila indeed had a plan. She wanted to pass close to the well in the city because she had a feeling that Sekhemib was looking for them. And, as the well was their meeting place, this seemed like a good idea to her. She would have liked to have asked Aiden for advice but she just couldn't risk the men becoming suspicious, so she kept doing what she planned. As soon as they arrived at the city borders the old chief ordered Akila to give the directions. She obeyed and prayed at the same time.

"Please let Sekhemib be there!"

Sekhemib woke up in the morning, rested but angry at himself that he had slept while the children might be in danger. He ran as fast as he could back to the city and went to every single place they had been together. He even went to the laundry area, but nowhere was there a sign of the children.

Sekhemib started to get desperate. What should he do now? Could it be that the children were abducted by some of his master's lackies? It was nearly noon by now and the heat was unbearable. The cat went back to the well at the market just so he could drink a bit of water and think about further steps. When Sekhemib arrived back at the well he got a real shock. The children were passing by riding on camels and in the company of a few men he thought could be nomads. The cat squinted its eyes and, without the men realising, followed the whole company.

Akila meanwhile felt so much better as she of course had been looking out for Sekhemib and, when she saw him, she felt just a tiny bit of hope that there was still a chance to get out of this situation in one piece. She elbowed Aiden and he also saw that the cat was following them.

The troop followed the girl in the direction she
was leading and soon they left the city westwards.
The landscape didn't look much different than
where they had come from but there were more
settlements outside of the city in this direction.
Small farms and huts near a dirt road led to the
Valley of the Kings a few miles away from the city.
The Valley of the Kings was the burial place of the
pharaohs and the girl was surprised that the men
didn't know the location of the pharaoh's future
resting place – but maybe her parents didn't tell her
everything. The location of the mausoleum her

parents were building for the pharaoh was a bit tricky though, she had to admit.

First, it was in one of the many caves already in the mountain, and second, it was still hidden from sight behind a huge stone rock. Only she knew that the rock could be moved quite easily, as her parents had been talented engineers, and had found a way to move heavy weights without a large amount of power. They had constructed the rock in just a few weeks and using it had concealed the entrance of the cave. Her parents had also found two caves, connected them to make a bigger space and then started building an impressive mausoleum inside. No one apart from her family and a few selected workers knew of the exact location and what was being built in there. Now Akila suspected that it was possibly no coincidence that her family and the workers were murdered on their way back to the city. Maybe someone had tried to find out where the mausoleum was and her family didn't want to give away the secret, as they obeyed their pharaoh's wishes. The girl's eyes filled with tears when she thought of her family and how she lost them just because they had been good builders. It wasn't fair that she and Aiden were also now in danger. She had a feeling that no matter how sweetly the old man spoke to them or how nicely he smiled, he was dangerous, and they had to find a way out of this mess.

Sekhemib tried to follow the caravan without the men realising. Though he was not one of the biggest cats of his breed, he still managed to keep up. It wasn't really a problem to hide in the city, but when the group left the towns borders he was aware that he had to be more careful. There were no houses or people around and the landscape changed quite quickly from the vegetation of the city to vast desert space. Nevertheless, he gave his best and, as the men were not looking out for a small animal following them, he managed to go unseen – at least for now.

After two hours of riding in the desert sun, the morning started to get warmer and the kids, especially Aiden, who wasn't used to this climate, felt uncomfortably hot. He whispered into Akila's ear, asking about when they would arrive and she whispered back quietly, "Soon." Akila didn't dare tell Aiden that she had seen Sekhemib in the city, and was hoping he had followed them and that he would somehow rescue them as well. She also didn't dare look behind to see if the cat was still there, just in case she alerted the men that they had a follower.

Soon afterwards the company arrived at the Valley of the Kings and the children were untied from the camel. Aiden felt quite stiff after this ride and he tried to stretch his sore muscles. The old man looked around impatiently and gave one of his men a nod. He came around and pushed Akila towards the chief. She nearly fell down and stumbled, tired from the journey and the exhaustion of too much excitement.

"So, which direction, little girl?" growled the old man without hiding his impatience and excitement.

Akila pointed into the direction of the bottom of the valley and the chief sighed.

"Typical. It couldn't be near the entrance, could it?"

And so the whole group started to climb down while a few men stayed with the camels. The valley was really hot and dusty, with no shadows to give a traveler a break from the desert sun. Akila and Aiden walked closely behind two men who led the group down the valley. After another hour they arrived at the bottom of the valley and made a stop.

"Now? Which way?" asked the old man, monosyllabic. He sounded as exhausted as the children felt. His friendly manners had completely vanished – gone was the smiling grandpa he had displayed the evening before.

"Tell me! Now!" he yelled, and the children were really startled.

Akila pointed, scared, to a big rock that was leaning against the mountain.

The chief's face went bright red and he shouted at the girl, "Are you kidding me? Where is the entrance?"

Aiden pressed Akila's hand and she walked up to the huge rock, touching, searching it's edges for something only she knew of. Her parents were immensely talented engineers and they had invented a mechanism that allowed one to move heavy objects like this rock just by pushing at an exact point. Even a kid like Akila could therefore move the rock: the rock turned around ninety degrees and exposed an entrance to a tunnel.

The men just stood there with their mouths open and couldn't believe what they were seeing. None of them would have thought it possible that the rock could be moved so easily or that there was even a tunnel behind it. It had just looked so perfectly aligned with the mountain that no one could have expected a secret entrance here.

The old man started to look feverishly around and bellowed orders to his men. One had to stay with the camels while the others had to look around for tree branches to make a provisional torch.

He got so impatient that he could not stop pacing around until his men were ready but, still, he sent the children into the tunnel first.

Akila and Aiden were holding again hands when they entered the tunnel. Though one of the men was close behind them and was holding a torch, the darkness somehow seemed to eat up the light that was shining from it. The children didn't dare to walk faster as they couldn't really see where they were going.

After a turn in the tunnel they nearly fell down stairs and if the man behind them had not held them back, they would have tumbled down.

The old chief yelled from behind, asking why they had stopped, and after a short discussion with the torch holder the children were pushed forwards. They stepped carefully down the stairway.

They felt like it was going downwards for ages and the children lost any sense of time. After what seemed to be an eternity they reached the end of the stairs and moved a bit forwards to let the others catch up. When the others arrived with the light of the other torches they saw that where they were standing was a huge cave with three tunnels leading in different directions.

The men looked confusedly around and the darkness and coldness of the cave made everyone shiver. Everything looked so empty and it was devoid of the usual carvings and paintings of graveyards that showed that a place belonged to a Pharaoh.

In all their excitement and fright the kids completely forgot about Sekhemib. All along the little temple cat had been following the group and, though he was now exhausted, he made his way down the path in the Valley of the Kings. He somehow managed to sneak into the cave entrance without the guard looking after the camels seeing him. Luckily he was able to find his way down the stairs without the need for light and his cat paws saved him from being heard by the men.

Soon he saw the lights of the torches and he stopped into the shadows of the stairs. The men seemed to argue about something, but he couldn't understand anything. The old chief was waving excitedly with his hands and pointed into the different tunnels leading away from the cave. His men all looked uncomfortable, and one even dared to shake his head in disagreement.

The old man's face went bright red with anger and he shouted at the young man, who flinched away and bent his head obediently.

"Now. We will split into three groups and each of the groups will investigate where the tunnels lead and then report back to me. You four take the left tunnel, you four the one on the right and the kids come with us into the middle tunnel. Come on, we have wasted enough time already!"

And so the group split up and went in different directions. Sekhemib again followed the children and their captors quietly, from quite a distance.

Akila never had been this far in the cave and tunnels as her parents had strictly forbidden her to go any further than the few metres at the tunnel entrance. She was scared and cold and her hand was clutching hard on Aiden's, which was shaking badly. He tried to comfort her but, each time, as soon as he would try to speak with her the old man would give Aiden a slap on the back of his head, so he stopped trying and just squeezed her hand once in a while. Aiden himself was beginning to doubt whether they were going to make it out of here unharmed.

Chapter VI   The Lion

The tunnel went on and on, and the kids felt it became darker with every step they made. Their steps echoed like a whole battalion were stomping through the tunnels and the noise felt deafening. All at once the tunnel stopped and there was nothing apart from a blank wall. No turn, no doorway nor anything else gave any indication that this was anything other than a dead end.

The chief started to swear and the children were mortified by his outburst. Akila tried to stand close to Aiden when her gaze fell on a little sign on the wall, near the bottom. It could have been easily overseen as just a scratch by anyone else, but she knew that this was the sign of her parents, a diagonal line with a dot underneath it.

"There." Akila pointed to the sign.

The old man turned around to gaze at the girl with his furrowed brows. He slowly walked towards her and nodded at her.

"Go on." He spoke quietly to her, which scared her even more than his outburst before.

Akila turned towards the sign and tried to remember everything her parents ever told her. Though she had never been this deep in the caves, she hoped she could open the entrance to the grave. Akila was certain that this was the entrance the men were looking for – but how to open it?

The girl let her hand move over the sign and then straight upward, looking for any trace of a lock or something similar. And there it was. A tiny little hole in the wall just a metre above the sign, only big enough to put a finger inside. She put her finger in the hole and just hoped that there wouldn't be any spiders hiding there. Akila tried to feel if there was anything like a hook or a button and, indeed, quite at the end of the hole she could feel a little button at her fingertip, which she pressed. A rumbling noise went through the cave and the wall started to shake as if an earthquake was tearing the ground apart. But nothing happened apart from the wall moving slowly upwards and giving way to another cave.

The chief went in first, followed by the children and his men. The light of the torches was thrown back multiplied when it fell on all the gold that was stashed in the cave. In the middle of the room was a huge stone sarcophagus and all around it there were shabti statues, the servants of the Pharaoh in the afterlife. At the foot of the sarcophagus were four canopic jars holding the organs of the mummy.

Everyone in the burial chamber was stunned by the riches that were stored here, and they were all only able to look around with surprised eyes. The chief opened his arms and turned around laughing, and his laugh went through the chamber like a thunder. Akila and Aiden nearly jumped, scared by the noise, and they were again holding hands.

"Get up and search the damn room you idiots!" yelled the chief at his men.

They stumbled apart like a group of chickens and started searching for something while the children looked on.

"Don't touch anything else, I want the bracelet. We can come again later and get whatever we want from here," he said, and he laughed maniacally.

Though the room was full of figurines, furniture and wonderfully painted boxes, the men were soon finished looking through all the things. They were not able to find a bracelet anywhere in the tomb and the chief started to get angry again.

"I know that it is here. The bracelet is a gift from the goddess Bastet given to this bastard in the tomb. I know it's here."

And with this he walked slowly towards the sarcophagus, stroking his beard.

"Well, well, damn me if the bracelet isn't still where it was when he was alive," the chief silently spoke to himself.

He ordered his men to open the sarcophagus and though they seemed to be reluctant, they obeyed him and moved the lid of the sarcophagus aside. The old man excitedly bent over and with a shriek ripped off a bracelet from the mummy's upper arm. And with the bracelet in his hand he turned around to look at the children while the men were already leaving the chamber tomb.

"Now my dear friends, thank you very much for your help."

"Will you let us go now?" asked Aiden – but the chief only laughed.

"I'm afraid, my young friends, I have explicit orders to not let you go anywhere. That's why I decided that you can stay here. Better to suffocate than to be eaten by wild animals, my friends. Fare well!"

He turned around, leaving the shocked children in the burial chamber while he pulled the handle at the side of the door.

Akila and Aiden heard his chuckles up until the door closed and only one torch was left for them, mocking their inability to escape from the darkness underground.

Akila started crying and Aiden couldn't do anything apart from hugging her. He couldn't think of anything comforting as he himself felt desperate as well. The children were holding each other while crying about being buried alive in the grave.

Sekhemib wasn't able to get into the chamber as the men would have seen him, so he was hiding in the shadows and cursing his inability to help the children.

After the men were gone, the cat tried everything to reach the little hole at the door to open it but there was nothing he could claw his fingers in and so he sat there in front of the door crying for the children inside.

While the men were already gone and on their way to their client, Sekhemib was still sitting in front of the door. And he cried and cursed and he started praying.

"Holy goddess Bastet. I am your humble servant. Please, help me. No, not me, but these innocent children who were caught up in my mistakes. Please. I beg you. Show mercy and help,"

and the cat cried and fell asleep, exhausted, on the floor.

The children were crying inside the chamber and they ,too, fell asleep: the journey had taken its toll on all of them.

The men, meanwhile, were riding on their camels as if someone was chasing them. They were hitting their camels to make them move faster and the poor animals were moaning and sweating because of the enormous effort they had to make. It was not long until the group saw the skyline of the city but they had to make a stop as the camels were so exhausted that they needed, at least for a little time, a bit rest.

The darkness in the tomb was scary as the torch had already burnt out, and the children did not know at first where they were – until the dreamworld slipped away completely and they realised that they were trapped in the pharaoh's tomb.

Sekhemib also woke up, outside the tomb – not because of the darkness but because there was a light coming down the stairs. The cat rubbed his eyes with his paws as he was not quite sure if he was still sleeping or if he was awake. The nearer the light came, the more Sekhemib thought he was still asleep. And then there stood before him a beautiful lion: so golden was his fur that it shone like the sun and brought light into the tunnel.

"Did you not call me, Sekhemib? Where are your manners? Don't you want to bow before your goddess, Bastet?"

And Sekhemib, still too confused to understand what the lion said, shook his head and murmured what a wonderful dream he was having, blessed be the goddess Bastet.

The lion started laughing and its laugh echoed like thunder from the walls. Only then did Sekhemib realise that the goddess was indeed in front of him, and he lay down immediately on the floor, shaking like a little kitten.

"Holy goddess Bastet. Forgive me, your humble servant, for being so blind. I gave up hope and hadn't dared to believe that you would hear my pleas."

"Rise, my dear Sekhemib. I am listening to all the prayers to me and your prayer is one of many. I do not, however, answer to all of them personally as you can imagine."

The lion chuckled as if it was telling a funny joke. Sekhemib, meanwhile, was sitting on his rear legs, still bowing his head.

"Look at me Sekhemib. I am here because those children are more important to this world than you know. I will not tell you more than this, as my interference might already anger the other goddesses and gods. But for now it's enough for you to know that we have to save and protect those two."

And Sekhmib stood up, still shaking, but his confidence strengthened by the assurance of the lion. He was grateful and mortified at the same time as, though he believed in the goddesses and gods, he never expected to know one until the day he actually died.

The lion-goddess turned around, looked at the closed entrance of the grave and gave out a roar so loud that the cat thought its eardrums were going to burst. Sekhemib had to close his eyes and when he opened them, the stone door was gone and there was only dust where the door had been before. The children were huddling together and their faces reflected their horror when they saw the lion.

Sekhemib hurried to get inside the chamber and tried to calm Aiden and Akila.

"I'm here. Everything is alright. Don't be scared. The lion is our goddess Bastet, and she came to help us. No worries, no worries, all will be well."

And the cat purred and head-bumped the kids, touching them with his tiny paws to loosen their paralysis. Very slowly the children were able to calm down and they started looking curiously at the lion, who sat there on her hind legs and cleaned herself while she waited for Sekhemib to bring the kids. She looked huge, and also quite bored, as if the worries of the kids were just a delay before the more important things that were to come.

"Come now, my dear little friends. We have to hurry. There's no time left to spare. We must get back to the city as grave danger may await us if we can't prevent the artefact being delivered to the temple. Come, come now," the lion urged the kids and their protector.

And the children and cat followed the lion out of
the grave and back to the entrance. There the
children looked helpless at the lion as the men had
taken the camels with them, seemingly leaving
them no choice but to walk back the whole way.
But the lion just shook its impressive mane and
roared as if it was laughing at some funny joke.

"Do you really think we could ever change fate if
we walked all the way back? I have other plans,
you see? On my back, little friends!"

The children climbed on the lions back and he stormed away, leaving Sekhemib in a dust cloud. The cat, having been very quiet the last few minutes, nodded to himself and mumbled.

"Maybe there is a chance after all."

And with a meow he followed the kids riding on the lion out the valley of death and towards the city.

Chapter VII   The Temple

The lion goddess, being so magical, ran as if the kids did not weigh anything and roared once in a while as if to warn everyone daring to come near to stay away. Sekhemib soon caught up but struggled to keep pace so the kids asked the lion for a break once in a while. Faster than the kids thought possible, the unusual group arrived at the city borders.

It was already night, stars sparkling all over the sky, and the citizens were back in their houses, keeping the cold of the desert outside.

No one saw the kids, riding on the back of a lion, accompanied by a temple cat. Maybe they would have just rubbed their eyes and thought for themselves that they got a sunstroke or maybe they would have run off, screaming and shouting, scared by what they seemed to see. But fortunately no one got robbed of their sleep and they arrived at the temple without having disturbed anyone in the city.

The children got off the lions back and both felt quite shaky after this exhausting ride and they tried to loosen their stiff muscles. Sekhemib, though a bit out of breath, paced around the kids, impatient to get inside and confront the temple head.

The lion goddess just stretched and started licking its paws.

So what are going to do now? Asked Akila and Aiden looked as lost as her.

We go inside and show this horrible cat who he is dealing with. Answered Sekhemib angry.

I doubt that this is a good idea to be honest. Aiden answered. We need a plan. We can't just go in and expect them to back off. Aiden started to pace up and down, his hands behind his back, like his father did when he was thinking about something. Just now Aiden felt very alone and wished his parents were here to help and advise him. He could not help it but a kind of desperation took hold of him and only Akila stopping him pacing up and down brought him back to reality. "No! I am not going to give up! Mum and Dad would want me to fight on." he thought for himself. Aiden straightened his shoulders and looked at his friends.

"I have an idea. But it won't be easy. And it will be dangerous. Are you all in?"

They all stood in a circle and though no one spoke, they looked in each others eyes, aware that this adventure could end badly. There was no guarantee that they would make it out of this in one piece but the children, the cat and even the goddess seemed to feel that the only way forward was to get into the temple and fight. No matter what the consequences. A strange group, ready to change their fate. And so Aiden shared with his friends the idea he had.

Slowly the children were creeping up to the entrance of the temple. They had to be careful and quiet as there were a few of the nomads standing outside and seemed to keep watch. The kids were huddling together around the corner and were watching the men, when Sekhemib just walked up the street to the temple, casually as if he was not in a rush at all, waving his beautiful tail from side to side. The men looked surprised at the cat, unsure what they should do, the sense of reverence towards temple cats keeping them from raising alarm. And Sekhemib, using this, sat down in front of the men, starting to clean his fur and licking his paws. The men turned towards him, watching fascinated while the cat went on with his business. That was the kids chance. Very quietly the children glided in to the temple entrance and vanished in the shadows.

While the children went inside and hid in the shadows, the goddess jumped around the corner, knocking over the men and Sekhemib followed Bastet into the temple. Inside they separated again, the children taking the left aisle while Sekhemib and the lion went on to the right.

The children tried to move on keeping in the shadows but the oil lamps scattered around the temple gave them away and halfway through the temple sanctuary they got caught by the nomads. Sekhemib and the lion watched in horror while the children got dragged away by the priests of the temple.

The temple chief looked utterly surprised when seeing the children and got agitated by their appearance. How indeed were they able to escape the tomb? They must have had help. But by whom?

Angrily he sent his helpers off to look after any more intruders. He turned around and looked again at the old nomad who was standing in-front of him and who had now a desperate look in his eyes.

"Give me the artefact!" The temple was nearly screaming.

"I will, as soon as you give me back my grandson or I swear I will destroy the artefact here and now. I have nothing to lose, you took away my son but I shall be damned if I let you have my son!" The old man looked the temple cat straight in the eyes and the cat was the first looking away.

The cat turned around and ordered his priests. "Very well then. Bring the boy here."

And after a moment the priests came back with a little boy of maybe five years, who looked frightened and confused. The child jumped and yelled. "Grandpa!"

The old man opened his arms and the child ran to him and jumped up and hugged him while crying. His grandfather closed his eyes when he slung his arms around the child.

"Now, if you please, would you be so kind and give me my artefact?" The temple cat asked acidly.

"Not that I want to disturb this family reunion but I'd be grateful if I could get on with my business!"

The old man gave a nod to one of his tribe and the man went out of the sanctuary to get the box where they stored the artefact. Soon he came back and handed the artefact to the temple cats priest.

The priest took the artefact and put it on the altar where already a golden bowl and an athame were placed.

The temple cat then screeched. "Out. Out. All of you. Get out!"

And everyone was hurrying out of the temple, stumbling over their own feet, scared of the erratic behaviour of the cat.

Only the children and the cats priests stayed in the room and even the priests looked afraid.

The cat started pacing up and down in-front of the alter, mumbling to himself, stopping once in a while and looking angrily at the children.

"Did you find anyone else here?" he asked his priests and all they could do was shook their head, scared that the temple cat would unleash his wrath on them.

"Bring the boy here!" he ordered and the priest holding Aiden dragged him along towards the altar. Aiden was kicking and pulling to get free but had no chance against the grown man holding him tight.

"You. You will be of use to me tonight. It is your own fault that you interfered with my plans but, at least you failed and now this will of use to me."

"Tie him up and put him on the alter!" he ordered the priest.

Akila was ashen when she realised what the temple cat was planning.

"No, no! Let him go!" and she started crying.

Aiden was soon lying on the alter, his hands tied up behind his back and he looked scared at Akila, who could not stop crying.

The temple cat jumped onto the alter, ordering the priests to take place on all four sides of the alter and they began a sing-sang the children did not understand. The cat had closed its eyes, swaying left and right to the rhythm of priests and when they ended their enchantments he yelled.

"Now! Kill him!" The priest held up high the athame and was just about to stab the boy when out of nowhere Sekhemib jumped on to the alter, intercepting the blade with his own little body.

The priest in his shock let go of the blade and ran off screaming like the other priests and then there were only Aiden, Akila, the temple cat and the dying Sekhemib left in the altar room. Akila hurried to Aidens side and removed the strings from his wrists and the kids walked around the alter towards the bleeding Sekhemib.

The children cried and stroked to the cats fur, not seeing their surroundings and not caring what the head of the temple cats was doing. He tried to sneak out of the room but found the exit blocked by the lion.

"You are not going anywhere!" the lion roared and the cat backed away into the room, terrified of the sight of a lion.

Bastet roared once more at the cat and shrieking the temple cat jumped away, hiding under a table in the corner, closing tight its eyes.

The children were still not paying any attention to their surroundings, overwhelmed by the grief of seeing their friend dying in-front of them. The goddess transformed and there stood instead of a lion a woman with the head of a cat.

Slowly she walked towards the altar and gently stroked over the grieving kids head. Both moved aside startled by the touch but too surprised by the goddess appearance.

"I think you both have suffered enough for today my dear little friends. Do not worry anymore." And she bend down here head, stroking slowly over the cats fur and then removing with one swift move the dagger out of the cats chest.

"You have sacrificed your life for a human being. You have shown bravery and courage beyond anything I would have ever expected from you and you have been honoured with the tears of those children who love you as if you would be one of them and who grieved for a true friend. For this I will gift you with a long life little one."

And she took the cat in her hands, lifted him up and let 3 drops of his blood drop into the golden bowl on the alter. Carefully she lay him down again on the alter and started the same sing-sang like the priest and when she was finished she took a stick, burned it on one of the oil lamps and put the burning stick into the bowl with Sekhemibs blood. Immediately smoke started to rise from the bowl, filling the whole room that the kids were not able to see anything anymore.

When the smoke waved away and the children were able to see their surroundings again, they gasped in horror as Sekhemib had vanished as well as the goddess.

Only a young man of maybe twenty, with olive skin and brown hair was lying on the altar no trace of the cat or the goddess.

The children walked slowly up to the alter, scared to death that their friend was dead and that this man had something to do with it.

But when they arrived at the altar and looked closer at the young man, he seemed familiar as if they had met him before. The young man opened slowly his eyes and Sekhemibs voice asked the children. "What has happened? Am I dead?" And the children realised that the goddess had transformed Sekhemib the cat into a human as a gift for his sacrifice in protecting Aiden.

Sekhemib himself looked stunned. He held up his hand in front of his face, turning his hand around, looking at it from all angles. And then he looked at the children, grabbed them both and hugged them till they could't breath anymore and started gasping for air. Then, only then he let them go and they laughed together tears of joy. The temple cat meanwhile tried to sneak out from under the table and to get out of the altar room but Sekhemib saw it and roared.

"Where do you think you are going, my friend?"

And he caught the cat and grabbed it on his neck and lifted it on the alter.

"Now, I am sure you want to help this boy and get out of here alive, don't you?" he asked the cat who was now shaking like a little kitten.

"Yes, yes, of course I am going to help. Anything you need, anything."

"Good, good. In that case I am expecting you to help us open the time portal so Aiden can return back to his time and life. That does sound fair to you, doesn't it?"

And the temple cat agreed to do everything Sekhemib wanted. Aiden was just worried if they would be able to send him exactly to the same time he came from but the temple cat just brushed off his concern.

"That is only a matter of an exact mathematical equation and we are good to go."

So they went all together to the chamber of the temple cat, to pick up all the ingredients for opening the time portal.

Akila meanwhile took the artefact from the altar room and together they left for the caves.

Aiden walked behind Sekhemib and the temple cat, beside Akila who was sniffing once in a while. He took Akilas hand, squeezed it and tried to comfort her.

"Look, you won't be alone anymore, you know that, right?"

Akila looked surprised at Aiden "Why would you think that?"

"Well, now that Sekhemib is a human, do you really think he would allow you to roam the streets at night and beg for food? You can bet on it that he will take care of you and you have to promise me that you will also take care of him, will you?"

And Akila promised Aiden that she would do that, while Sekhemib smiled as he still had the hearing of a cat and had heard everything the boy had said.

No later then midnight they arrived at the caves and they arranged everything for the ritual. The cat was sitting in front of the alter, mumbling to itself about numbers and calculations, while Sekhemib put all the ingredients on to the altar.

Aiden then went up to him and asked him to go up to the cave entrance.

"Sekhemib, I… I just wanted to say thank you."

"For what? For endangering you? For putting you through hunger, darkness and fright? I am sorry, I am so sorry that I was not careful and that I put you through all of this. Please forgive me my friend." And he fell on his knees and hugged the boy.

"No. Thank you for showing me this time, showing me what real friendship means and for saving my life. I will never forget you!" And the boy hugged him back and cried till the cat called from the other end of the cave.

Sekhemib stood up and went after a last look at Aiden towards the altar, when Akila came to stand beside Aiden. They looked out from the cave entrance, watching the myriads of stars twinkling on the black sky and for a moment the held hands, saying their quiet goodbyes.

Sekhemib called the children and they walked hand in hand to the altar.

"It is time, my dear friend." Sekhmib said and in that moment a bright light appeared out of nowhere, burning like a little flame and growing bigger and bigger.

"You have to go through it." Sekhemib whispered and gave the boy a little push towards the light.

Aiden turned around and wanted to say something, seeing his friends standing there, hand in hand, but a pull from the light so strong that he was not able to resist it, sucked him in and he yelled.

"No, I don't want to go. You are my friends." But the light became so bright, he had to close his eyes and when he opened them, his friends were gone.

Epilogue

They did it. Aiden couldn't believe they managed to open the time portal. He was going home. Oh, how he missed his parents. What would they say when they saw him? Would they be upset? Or just happy to have him back? With these thoughts, Aiden walked towards the portal and through the blinding white light.

This couldn't be right. Aiden looked around, confused, when he stepped out of the portal. What was going on here? This couldn't be right, there must have been a mistake or perhaps he landed at the wrong time, or something else. It was broad daylight and the noise from the street was deafening. Everywhere people were walking around, cars were on the streets, and Aiden could see children with their parents walking on the pavements, laughing, singing, talking. The buildings were perfectly fine, no debris, no empty, barricaded buildings, the streets were paved and devoid of any holes. There were trees, grass, flowers, and Aiden was just standing there, he couldn't stop looking. The entrance of the church where he was standing was empty of all the broken gravestones he remembered from a week earlier, but it looked like the same place just completely fine. What was going on? He heard the door behind him open and an old priest came out of the church.

"Excuse me, sir, I mean Father – can you please tell me where I am?"

"Are you lost, my boy?"

"I am not sure, sir..."

"This is the Trinity Church at 78th street."

"In New York City?"

"Yes, in New York City. You sure you are not lost? I can call your parents, if you want. I wouldn't want you to wander around alone here."

"Sir, what year is it?"

"It is 3707. The whole year already."

"Thank you, sir."

"My boy, I think we really should call your family, you seem to be a bit confused..."

"No sir, I'm fine. Everything is alright, really. I'm just going home now."

And with this Aiden started to walk down the stairs and when he reached the pavement he started to run and run and run till he arrived breathless at his street. Everything looked completely different. The houses were well looked after, no broken windows, no burned out cars. It reminded Aiden of the pictures from the early 21st century he had seen, when everything was still alright, people were healthy, kids were healthy, where bees still existed. What was going on?

Aiden walked towards their house. Would his parents be still there? What if they didn't live here anymore? It was the correct time he came back to, but what if they didn't exist? Aiden became a bit scared now, as he walked up the stairs to the front door. Just when he reached out for the door knob, the door swung open and his mother looked at him surprised.

"Aiden, where have you been? We were getting worried when you didn't come back in time from school. My dear son, I think we have to talk about keeping an eye on the clock, don't we?"

Aiden couldn't hold himself back and threw himself around his mother's neck and hugged her so tight that she cried out in agony.

"Aiden! You're hurting me. What is going on?"

"Mum, I missed you so much!"

That was all Aiden could say for a while and he just cried hugging his mum. She looked surprised and worried but did hold her son tight until he stopped crying.

"Are you feeling better now?"

"Much. Thank you."

"How about I make you a hot chocolate and you can rest in your room a bit? Does that sound like a good idea? And then you can tell me why you cried."

"Yes mum. It does."

Aiden walked slowly into his room while his mum watched him in disbelief and worry. He would need to explain himself to her later but Aiden had a bigger problem right now. He had to find out what had happened the last week and why the future, or to be precise, his present, had changed.

When Aiden came into his room, he nearly didn't recognise it. There where bookshelves and posters, and a table with a chair, a whole box with cars and other toys, stuffed toys all over his bed, and there was even a computer on his table. Aiden looked around with awe and couldn't believe that it was his room, but it must have been as there were pictures of him in frames on his bedside table, as well as on the walls. Him with a baseball team, him with a swimming team, a picture of a whole class, one with his parents. It was as if he had entered someone else's life. Aiden sat down at the table and turned on the computer, which he had learned to use at school – he needed to find out what had changed. He typed "Ancient Egypt" in a search engine but there didn't seem any changes as far as Aiden could see.

He looked for the history of the 21st century and there it was. Bees dying out. A bacteria, produced by a group of terrorist biologists using an artefact from Ancient Egypt for the purpose of blackmailing countries all over the world, mutated and killed bees. Academics and leading biologists from every single country were trying their best to stop the bacteria from spreading, but the samples they had of the original bacteria strain were stolen. Only after they discovered a new grave in the Valley of the King's did they find the strain again, and they were able to create an antidote which saved the bees. That was it. Akila's knowledge about the exact position of the king's grave and the fact that Sekhemib and Akila must have brought back the artefact to its rightful place, made it possible for the historians to find it in the 21st century and therefore to save the bees and humanity. With his time travel Aiden had changed the past and therefore saved the future by helping to find a cure. This was a good day indeed.

24072204R00073

Printed in Great Britain
by Amazon